Hans Christian Andersen's

The Snow Queen

Retold by
Geraldine McCaughrean

Illustrated by
Laura Barrett

For Toby
- *G. McC.*

For my grandad, the painter,
and for Kay with the warm heart
- *L. B.*

ORCHARD BOOKS

First published in Great Britain in 2019
by The Watts Publishing Group
The artwork on pages 6, 8, 11, 12,
17, 18 and 20 was first published in
concertina format in 2018

10 9 8 7 6 5 4 3 2 1

Text © Geraldine McCaughrean, 2019
Illustrations © Laura Barrett, 2018, 2019

The moral rights of the author and
illustrator have been asserted.

ISBN 978 1 40835 234 2

MIX
Paper from
responsible sources
FSC
www.fsc.org
FSC® C104740

Printed and bound in China

Orchard Books
An imprint of Hachette Children's Group
Part of The Watts Publishing
Group Limited
Carmelite House
50 Victoria Embankment
London EC4Y 0DZ

An Hachette UK Company
www.hachette.co.uk

www.hachettechildrens.co.uk

ORCHARD

Hans Christian Andersen's
The Snow Queen

Retold by
Geraldine McCaughrean

Illustrated by
Laura Barrett

Long, long before you were born,

a gaggle of goblins made a magic mirror to admire their
silly selves. They made it of mischief and shining ice.
But as they fought to see themselves –

"Me first! Me first!"

– the mirror spun from their hands,
still holding their horrid reflections.

It smashed into tiny slivers. The winds swallowed them
up and swept them around the round world, where their
sharp magic jabbed and stabbed loving hearts and
froze the good inside them.

Summer is lovely with its hazy, lazy days,
its golden swarms of bees. Gerda and Kai would sit among the
roses on neighbouring balconies, talking and telling stories.
The two friends loved each other dearly and –
can you believe it? – they *never* quarrelled.

❄

But summer never stays long. Winter soon returns,
bringing frost-glitter windows and silver swarms of snow.
Cosy in Grandma's kitchen, Kai liked to peer out at the
shining, slippery streets, the skaters and snowballs flying.

One day, someone looked back.

"That must have been the Snow Queen," said Grandma. "The fiercest blizzard and the tiniest snowflake belong to her. They say she is as lovely as any snowflake – and as cruel as any blizzard."

Kai peeped out, wanting another glimpse of the queen but –

"Ow, That hurt!" Something sharp stung his eye.

Gerda rushed to help, but –

"Ow, my chest!" The sliver of goblin mirror had already lodged in Kai's heart.

From that moment, Kai was full of goblin mischief . . . and empty of joy. He was rude to Grandma and unkind to Gerda. He sulked and sneered and, instead of doing as he was told, he did as he liked, went where he wanted. Out and about. Alone.

And when, in the market square, he saw the beautiful lady again,
in her curlicue silver sleigh, he just climbed in beside her. Had to.
Something made him. A magic bigger than mischief.

"A little ride?" she said.

But a trot became a gallop. The town lights were left behind.
The sleigh lifted into the air, high into the sky, and flew over
rivers, over trees, over lands, over seas and beyond.

"*Maybe he fell in the river!*" people said, after
Kai disappeared. So, sobbing, Gerda ran there, and
stepped into a bobbing boat. It carried her downstream,
all the way to the cottage of a gentle witch.

The witch enjoyed sunshine all year round in her magic
garden. But she was lonely. The moment she saw sweet,
kind Gerda, she longed to keep the girl. For ever.

But the roses in the witch's garden made Gerda remember
happy days with Kai . . . and remembering made her cry.
So, as the witch dried Gerda's tears, she wiped away her
memories too. And just in case the roses should fetch the
memories back, she banished them from her garden.

Gerda spent her days playing. The witch's flowers told her their silly, sleepy dreams. The birds twittered about far-off places. The witch was so happy with her lovely little girl that she even put on her "happy hat" – the one with cloth roses round the brim. Seeing those roses, Gerda remembered everything.

"Kai! Grandma!"

Away she ran, out of the gate, out of magical summertime, barefoot and without a coat. "Oh, help me find Kai!" she called to the birds overhead.

"Not so long ago," said Clever Crow, "a lad came to a palace close by and married a princess there. A handsome lad with squeaky boots."

"Oh, that is Kai for certain sure! Show me, Crow! Show me where!"

And he did. Over high gates, past sleepy guards, up winding stairs to a tall turret crept Gerda, with only the moon for a torch. There lay the prince, sleeping under a moonbeam. Such a handsome face, but . . .

Not Kai!

Gerda's unhappy wail woke the prince and princess.

They might have called, "Guards! Arrest this ragamuffin!"
But no. They listened to her sad story and dried her eyes.

Next morning, they gave her warm gloves and a cloak, money,
a coach and horses. *"Find him. Find Kai!"* they said.
"Love is too wonderful to lose!"

Bowling along in that royal coach,
Gerda looked quite like a princess herself.

The robbers really thought she was one . . .
Lying in wait in the dark forest, they ambushed her and
took her coat and coach and money. They might have killed her . . .
but for their little robber daughter.

"Give her to me! I want-want-want her for a pet!"

The little Robber Girl was not kind to any of her many pets. But she
want-want-wanted stories, so Gerda told her of her search for Kai, and the
girl found herself want-want-wanting to help.

Robbers listen in. Robbers listen out.
Robbers pick the world's pockets for information.
One day the Robber Girl came home triumphant with news:

"The Snow Queen has taken Kai north in her sleigh!"

For the first time ever, she *gave* instead of *taking* –
gave Gerda her freedom and a pet reindeer
to ride to the country of coloured skies.

Towards the top of the world they rode, curtains of drifting light colouring the sky . . . but Gerda was so cold and tired that she barely noticed them. Clinging tight to the reindeer's antlers, she galloped on until at last she came to a house.

Those lights in the sky must drip wisdom, because the woman who lived there was wonderfully wise. She knew a sweet, kind girl when she saw one. And she knew the way to the Snow Queen's palace.

"But when I get there, how will I set Kai free?" said Gerda.

Buttering toast, simmering soup, making up a bed,
the wise woman sang:

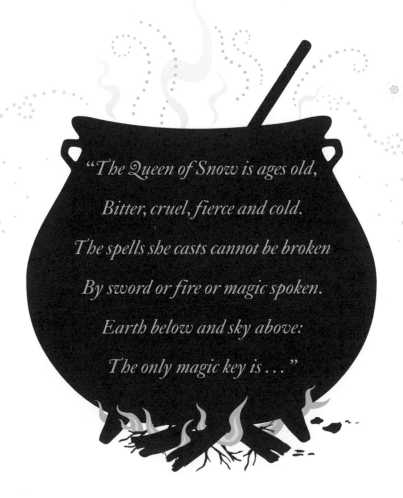

"The Queen of Snow is ages old,

Bitter, cruel, fierce and cold.

The spells she casts cannot be broken

By sword or fire or magic spoken.

Earth below and sky above:

The only magic key is . . . "

Then she smiled and kissed Gerda. "I believe you have all the magic you need. Now, you must simply find the courage . . . "

The palace of the Snow Queen is all ice. The winds
have carved it into spires, domes and high halls.

The Snow Queen sits now on her throne, watching her prisoner.

"Try, Kai! Try! When the puzzle is solved, you can leave."

But Kai's mind is numb with cold. His heart is hardly beating. His hands are blue, his eyes empty. The pieces of the puzzle are splinters of ice, sharp as broken windowpanes, and he must shape them into a word. The Snow Queen watches him shiver and smiles.

Then, in a flurry of fur, she throws on her cloak and leaps aboard her sleigh. It is half past February and time to sprinkle snow on the volcanoes of Quetzapulco.

"Try, Kai! Try!" she calls, though she knows he will fail.

The silver sleigh swoops over, but Gerda holds very still, like a mouse when the owl is hunting. With the queen gone, she creeps into the palace, footsteps echoing, teeth chattering.

And there is her dear Kai!

He is crouched on the ice of a great frozen lake, stiff and
blue with cold. She runs and hugs him, tugs on his arm . . .

But Kai won't move – can't move. "I must solve the puzzle!"

Gerda glances down. "But that's easy!"

Oh, Gerda! Kai! Look out!
The Snow Queen is coming back!

The word takes shape. Kai stares. His heart thaws and fills
with love. His fear melts. His fingers can feel again.

But outside, white wolves are howling. They have seen
whose sleigh blades are slicing through the snow.

Gerda and Kai run. Waiting in the snow is
Gerda's reindeer, who has found a friend too.

Gallop, little reindeers! Run like the wind!

South towards spring they travel,
Gerda, Kai, their two brave reindeer. No angry blizzard
chases them. The Snow Queen is left far behind.

They stop to thank the wise woman, tiptoe past the
robbers' den, visit the prince and princess in their palace,
and wave to the witch as they row past her cottage.

Finally the city greets them.

"Can it be? Can it really be you?" cries Grandma.
Below her window, the roses are coming into bud.

Life lies ahead, as lovely as before . . . except – and here's odd –
Gerda and Kai seem older, as if they have been gone for years.

Maybe they have. But young or old, one thing will never change: the love between them – bright as roses – will last all year round and evermore.